I Hate To Wait

By Sigal Adler

Young Harry Monster has waited all year,
And now Halloween is almost here.
He knows just what he wants to be,
A pirate — the terror of the high sea!

He spotted a costume in the store,
One time when he was there before.
With a big bandana and a sword,
He'd rule his mighty pirate horde.

But when he gets there, feeling fine—
Poor Harry spots a long, long line!
If there's one thing that monsters hate,
It's line-ups—they can't stand to WAIT!

"Get in line," the others mumble.
Standing there, he starts to grumble.

But what can our young Harry do?
He wants that costume, shiny new.
What if someone buys it first?
Oh, that would be the very worst!

Hoping he can reach his goal,
He thinks that he can take control.
"Out of my way!" he yells aloud,
Shoving past the busy crowd.

But no-one moves or lets him through,
"We were here ahead of you!
We're not afraid of what you do—
And we want to buy costumes, too!"

And then he's shocked: a girl so young,
Turns around and sticks out her tongue.

Though shouting didn't help one bit,
Harry knows he just can't quit.
He calls, "Hey, you! Out of my way!
I'll stomp your feet to make your day!"

But nobody moves out of the line,
"We're not scared, even if you whine!
No matter how you yell and fuss,
You'll have to wait like all of us!"

And then he's shocked: a grandma so old
Stomps on HIS foot — so quick and so bold!

He doesn't believe it—what can he do?
He's waited a year for his dream to come true.
He wants to dress up and celebrate,
But now he has to stand and wait!

Nothing is working! He wants to go fast!
But nobody's moving to let him go past.
Frustrated and sad, tears roll down his cheeks,
Thinking he won't get the costume for weeks!

As he waits, Harry watches the others.
Fathers and sons, sisters and brothers.
One girl tries on a witch's long cape,
Swishing around, a most fearsome shape.

One boy chooses a sleek suit to try,
With a cape and a mask — he might even fly!
That kind of costume might really be great,
But a pirate is better, so Harry must wait.

Poor Harry is desperate — what can he do?
He NEEDS that costume, he's got to get through!
There's just one strategy he hasn't tried—
Talking to people to tell them his side.

So Harry tells them, all honestly,
About the pirate he's hoping to be.
How he got up early that morning, at dawn
And he's scared the costumes will all be gone!

"Could you please help me?" those people hear,
As Harry asks nicely, sounding sincere.
He understands now, without any doubt.
That he never really had to shout.

Someone takes Harry by the hand
To ask a man who'll understand.
The manager quickly takes charge
And finds one costume—Extra Large!

Harry thanks him with a smile,
Happy now to wait a while.
"I don't mind standing in line
To make that awesome costume mine!"

So Harry waits there in that crowd,
Thinking of how he'll feel so proud.
He didn't have to scream or hit...
And it's Extra Large, a perfect fit!

When Halloween comes, Harry acts so mean,
The fiercest pirate you've ever seen.
He shouts and stomps and scares his friends,
And loves every minute until the day ends.

But most of the year, he's learned to be nice,
Speaking respectfully and asking advice.
Yelling and stomping just aren't polite,
Except once a year on Halloween night!

Happy Halloween

For More Books by

SIGAL ADLER

VISIT
FACEBOOK.COM/COM.PG.SIGALADLERBOOKS